THIS WALKER BOOK BELONGS TO:

_____

_____

_____

For My Very Own Father – who, if he were a dog, would
of course be a most intelligent, witty and dignified breed.
E. B.

For Dad, of course! And the dogs, as with every dog
I have ever drawn, are for Mum.
R. C.

First published 2006 by Walker Books Ltd
87 Vauxhall Walk, London SE11 5HJ

This edition published 2007

2 4 6 8 10 9 7 5 3 1

Text © 2006 Elizabeth Bluemle
Illustrations © 2006 Randy Cecil

The right of Elizabeth Bluemle and Randy Cecil to be identified as author and illustrator
respectively of this work has been asserted by them in accordance
with the Copyright, Designs and Patents Act 1988

This book has been typeset in SoupBone

Printed in China

British Library Cataloguing in Publication Data:
a catalogue record for this book
is available from the British Library

ISBN 978-0-7445-9391-4

www.walkerbooks.co.uk

My Father the Dog

Elizabeth Bluemle illustrated by Randy Cecil

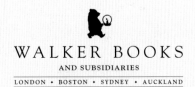

WALKER BOOKS
AND SUBSIDIARIES
LONDON · BOSTON · SYDNEY · AUCKLAND

My father pretends to be human,
but I know he is really a dog.

Consider the evidence:

When he wakes up, he starts off the day with a good scratch.

He fetches the newspaper every morning.

My father loves playing tug-of-war ...

but he hates losing.

In the car, he likes the windows down
and the breeze on his face.

He has been known to nip behind the bushes...

My father can lie around for hours.

He growls when you wake him up.

If you throw a ball, he'll chase after it.

My father loves snacks.

I've never actually seen him begging for leftovers under the kitchen table, but it might happen.

When he toots, he looks around
the room like someone else did it.

He is good at looking innocent when
he knows he's done something wrong.

If he hears a noise in the middle of the night, he runs downstairs to investigate.

My father loves us all and thinks
we're the best family in the world ...

which is good, because Mum says we can keep him.

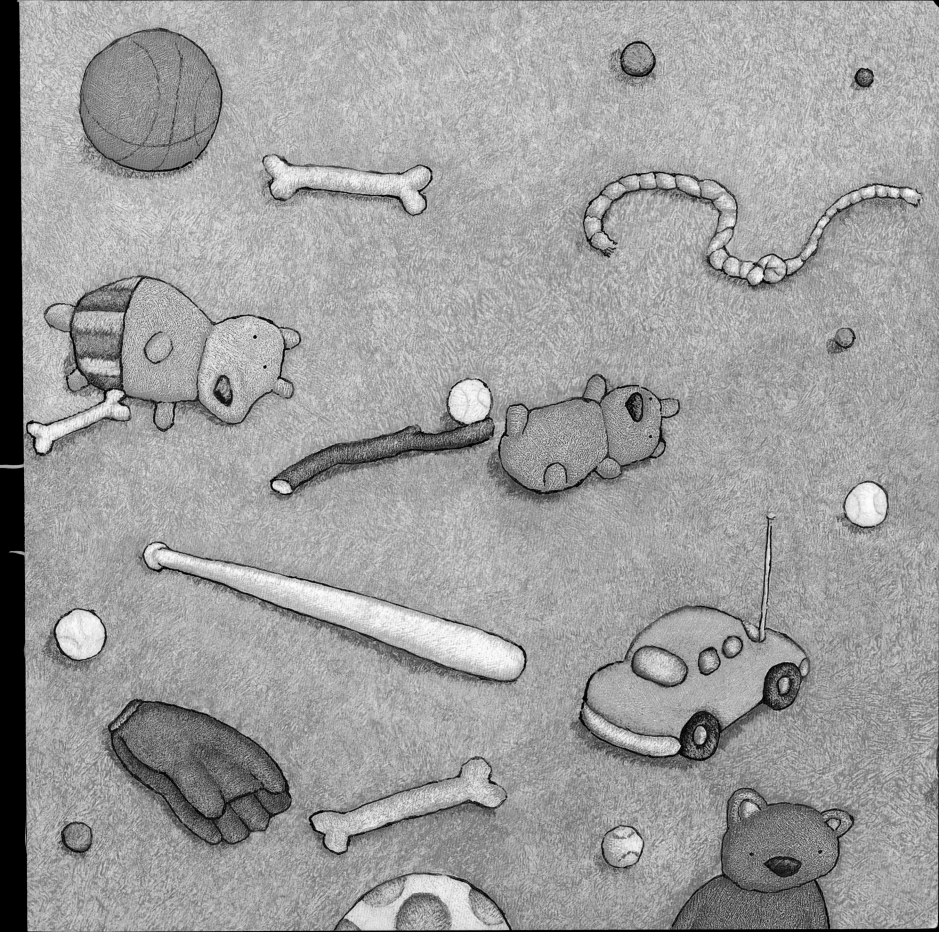

WALKER BOOKS is the world's leading independent publisher of children's books. Working with the best authors and illustrators we create books for all ages, from babies to teenagers – books your child will grow up with and always remember. So…

FOR THE BEST CHILDREN'S BOOKS, LOOK FOR THE BEAR